FLAGS OF THE WORLD

Activity Book

ARCTURUS

ARCTURUS

This edition published in 2019 by Arcturus Publishing Limited
26/27 Bickels Yard, 151–153 Bermondsey Street,
London SE1 3HA

Author: Annabel Savery
Designer: Elaine Wilkinson
Illustrator: Hui Skipp, with additional images from Shutterstock and BigStock
Editor: Sebastian Rydberg

ISBN: 978-1-78950-598-6
CH007140NT
Supplier 29, Date 0919, Print run 8269

Printed in China

CONTENTS

WHAT ARE FLAGS?

Have you seen a flag flying outside an important building, or on top of a boat, or held up at the start of a sports competition? Flags are designed to represent countries, places, teams, and organizations.

Flags are usually rectangular, but they can be other shapes, such as squares or triangles. They have bright, simple designs so that they can be recognized from far away. Countries in the same region often have similar flags.

Red, white, and blue are used in many European flags, but also by many countries in Southeast Asia.

Croatian flag

Laotian flag

Many flags are divided into sections using stripes, triangles, or crosses.

French flag

An emblem is a picture or symbol that represents a country or organization. The maple leaf is the emblem of Canada.

Canadian flag

A coat of arms is a set of symbols put together in a shield or other design. They were once put on soldiers' shields in battle. Now they represent countries, organizations, or families.

IN THIS BOOK

This book shows you the flags of all the independent countries in the world. Read through the information pages and complete the flags, then have a go at the puzzle pages to test your knowledge!

Each chapter looks at the countries in each continent as shown on the map below:

- Europe
- North and Central America
- Asia
- Africa
- South America
- Oceania

The study of flags is called "vexillology." The name comes from a Roman cavalry flag called the vexillum.

EUROPE

Denmark

Denmark has one of the oldest monarchies in the world, and one of the oldest national flags. Their flag is known as the *Dannebrog*, which means "Danish cloth."

Greenland is a territory of Denmark. It uses the red and white of the Danish flag but the design represents sun and ice.

Complete the Danish flag.

Sweden

The Swedish flag is inspired by the coat of arms, which shows a blue shield with three gold crowns. The three crowns represent the "three wise kings" and have been used by Sweden since the 14th century.

Norway

Norway gained independence in 1905, having been part of Denmark and then under Swedish rule. They kept the design of the Danish flag but added a blue stripe. The design was influenced by the French *Tricolore* and the flags of the USA and UK.

Together, Sweden, Norway, and Denmark are known as Scandinavia. Their national flags share the Scandinavian cross.

Iceland

For a long time, Iceland was ruled by Denmark. It became a republic in 1944. The design uses blue for the ocean, white for the ice and snow, and red for the island's fiery volcanoes.

Finland

The Finnish flag represents white snow and blue of the skies and many lakes. This flag has been used since Finland became an independent nation in 1917, having been part of the Russian Empire.

Belgium

The Belgian flag is designed from the country's coat of arms: Black from the shield, yellow from the lion, and red from the lion's tongue and claws.

Netherlands

The red stripe in the Dutch flag was originally orange. It was changed to red in the 17th century. The orange had been a tribute to William of Orange, who led the movement for independence from Spanish rule.

Try your own Union Jack!

Ireland

The flag of the Republic of Ireland was first used in 1848 by the movement for independence for Ireland. It became the official national flag in 1937 when Ireland became an independent nation.

The Irish *tricolore* is made up of green, orange, and white. The Green represents the Catholic people, the orange represents the Protestant people, and the white represents peace between the two faiths.

United Kingdom

The flag of the United Kingdom represents the countries of England, Wales, Scotland, and Northern Ireland. The union between England, Scotland, and Wales was formed in 1707. The flag is commonly known as the Union Jack.

LETTER LAND

Can you unscramble these letters to spell the country names?

A DWESNE

B LIFANND

C DINECAL

D YARNOW

E KANEMRD

Without looking back at the page before, can you remember how to complete each flag?

MEMORY TEST

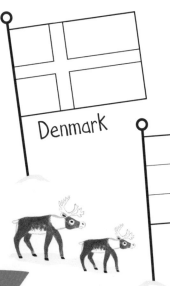
Denmark

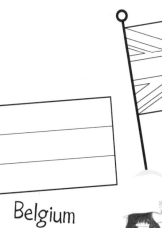
Belgium

UK

Ireland

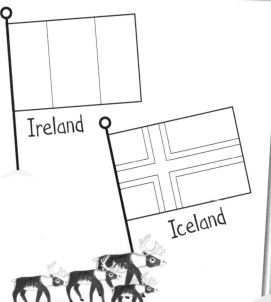
Iceland

PATCH IT UP

These flags have been snipped into pieces. Can put them back together?

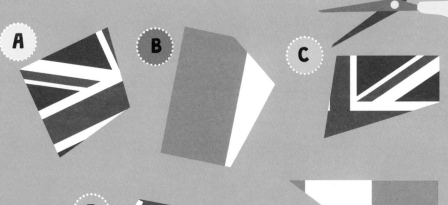

A B C

D E F G

UP IN ARMS

Here is the coat of arms of Belgium. Can you copy the original?

Use the shield to design your own coat of arms.

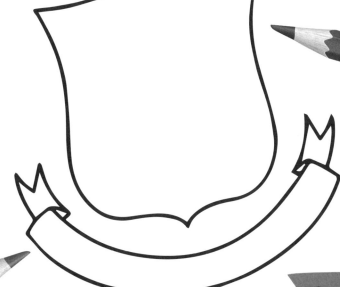

France

The French flag is known as the *"Tricolore."* It is one of the best known "three-stripe" designs. Blue and red are said to stand for Paris, while white represents the royal House of Bourbon.

The *Tricolore* was used in the French Revolution of 1789. The flag came to represent the ideals of *liberté, egalité et fraternité*—"freedom, equality, and solidarity."

Create your own Tricolore!

Monaco

Monaco is a tiny state on the south coast of France. It has been ruled over by the Grimaldi family since 1297. They were originally from Genoa in Italy.

Monaco uses the coat of arms of the Grimaldi House. Two monks with raised swords stand next to a white shield decorated with red diamonds.

Andorra

Andorra is a small principality in the Pyrenees mountains, between France and Spain. The flag shares the red and yellow of the Spanish flag, and the red and blue of the French flag. Through history, the two bigger nations have protected the smaller state.

A principality has a prince as the head of state.

Portugal

Portugal is historically a great seafaring and exploring nation. Their emblem shows an armillary sphere and a shield. The armillary sphere is a tool that was once used on ships.

Spain

The Spanish flag was designed to make Spanish ships stand out at sea— as no other nation were using red and yellow. On the yellow stripe is the Spanish coat of arms.

Castile
Aragon
Léon
Navarre

The arms of Spain are designed to show each of the regions of Spain.

San Marino

The small republic of San Marino is built on the slopes of Mount Titano. On the flag, blue represents the sky and the white the clouds above the peak.

The coat of arms shows three castles, and around the edge are laurel and oak branches.

Malta

The flag of Malta shows a George Cross in the top left corner. This is a military medal. It was awarded to the Maltese people by King George VI for their bravery in World War II.

Luxembourg

The flag of Luxembourg is similar to the Dutch flag, but the blue is lighter. It is inspired by the Grand Duke's arms: A blue and white striped background, with a red lion on top.

Complete Luxembourg's flag.

Italy

When French military commander Napoleon brought his troops to conquer northern Italy, he brought the French flag too! The Italian *Tricolore* has green in place of blue.

Napoleon Bonaparte went on to become Emperor Napoleon, one of the most famous military leaders in history!

WIN THE RACE!

Follow the tangled lines to see which country's race car reaches the black and white flag first!

TWO HALVES

Half of each flag is missing—can you complete them?

A Malta

C Luxembourg

B Monaco

D France

BUBBLE TROUBLE

These bubbles show sections of four flags. Can you guess where each bubble comes from?

A

B

C

D

Clues on page 10-11

QUICK QUIZ!

How much can you remember about the flags on pages 10–11?

1. Which military general brought the three-stripe flag to Italy?

2. What award was given to the people of Malta?

3. Why is there an armillary sphere on the flag of Portugal?

4. Why were red and yellow chosen for the Spanish flag?

5. What country is built on the slopes of Mount Titano?

Germany

The German flag was designed in 1848 when Germany was divided into many separate states. This design became the official nation flag in 1990 when East and West Germany re-united.

Poland

The red and white of the Polish flag are taken from the country's coat of arms: A white eagle on a red field (background).

Poland's eagle emblem has been used since the 12th century.

Switzerland

Switzerland is made up of 26 areas called cantons. The Swiss flag design was taken from the flag of Schwyz, one of the first three cantons that joined together to form the country.

Complete the Swiss flag.

Czech Republic

The Czech Republic and Slovakia were one nation, Czechoslovakia, until 1993. The blue triangle was added to the flag to make it different from Poland's.

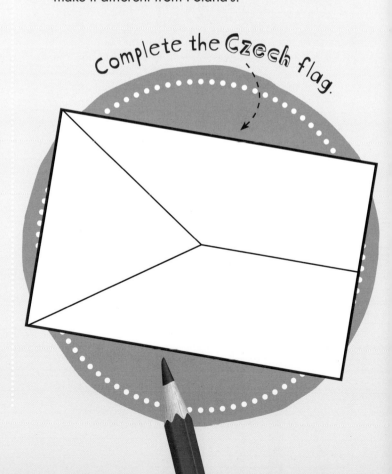

Complete the Czech flag.

Liechtenstein

The flags of Liechtenstein and Haiti caused confusion at the 1936 Berlin Olympics because they were so similar. In 1937, Liechtenstein added a gold crown to their flag. Now you can tell the two apart!

Complete the crown.

Hungary

The Hungarian flag was designed by revolutionaries 1848. They wanted independence for Hungary from the vast Austrian Habsburg empire. They used red to represent strength, white for faith, and green for hope.

Slovakia

Slovakia formed part of Czechoslovakia until 1993 when it became independent. The flag shows the arms of Slovakia: A white double cross and blue mountains, on a red background.

Complete the Slovakian flag.

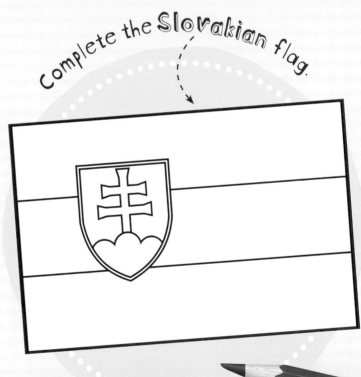

Austria

The red-white-red pattern has been used by Austria for 800 years. The Austrian government flag also has a black eagle with a hammer and a sickle in its claws.

The hammer represents industry, and the sickle represents agriculture.

THREE TO FIND

Can you find these three flags in this order, in the grid opposite?

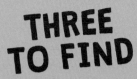

Can you fill in the blank flags with the correct flag to fit the pattern?

A

B

C

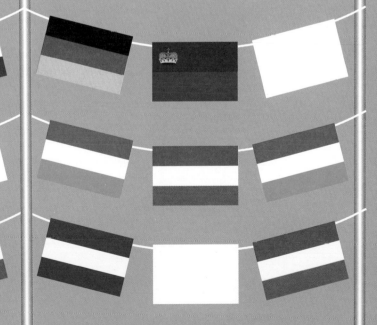

16

PAINT THE FLAG

Link each flag with the correct paint palette. Then name the country!

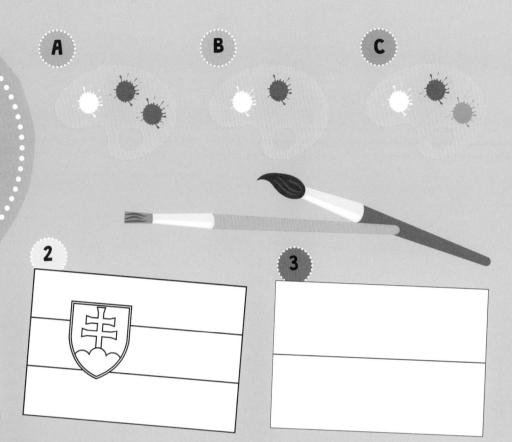

A   B   C

1

2

3

NUMBER CRUNCHING

Can you solve the Austrian flag sudoku?

There is a traditional story of an Austrian duke who was involved in such a fierce battle that his tunic was stained with blood. When he removed his sword belt, a white stripe of material remained. He took the pattern of red and white stripes to be his emblem.

		3		1	
5	6		3	2	
	5	4	2		3
2		6	4	5	
	1	2		4	5
	4		1		

Slovenia

The Slovenia flag has the same three stripes as Slovakia's: White, blue, and red. The coat of arms shows mountains, the sea, and three gold stars.

Complete the Slovenian flag.

Croatia

The Croatian flag uses the Pan-Slav combination of red, white, and blue. The coat of arms shows a red and white check shield, with five small shields above it. Each of these represents a region of the country.

Montenegro

Until 2006, Montenegro and Serbia were one state. When they separated, Montenegro designed their flag around one first used in the 1880s. Their coat of arms shows the double-headed eagle and a lion.

Complete the emblem.

Bosnia and Herzegovina

White, blue, and yellow were chosen for the Bosnia and Herzegovina flag as they traditionally stand for peace. The triangle represents the shape of the country and also the country's three ethnic groups—Bosniaks, Croats, and Serbs.

The stars on the Bosnia and Herzegovina flag represent Europe.

Romania

Romania became independent from the Ottoman Empire in 1859. The flag shows the blue and red of the old Wallachia province, and the yellow and red of the old Moldavia province.

Moldova

Moldova has been independent since 1991. Moldova was once joined with Romania and their flags are still similar. The arms of Moldova are in the central stripe of their flag.

The arms of Moldova show an eagle holding a cross. On the shield is an ox head, a rose, a crescent, and a star.

Complete the Romanian flag.

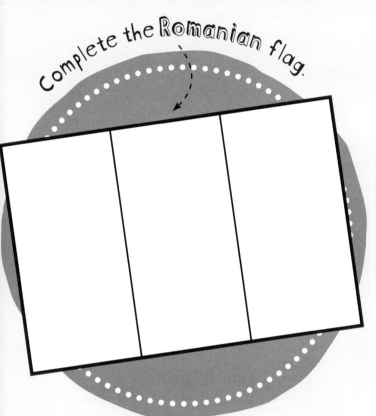

Ukraine

Ukraine's flag was first used in 1918 when it first became independent. It was then controlled by the Soviet Union until 1991. The flag shows yellow wheat fields and blue skies.

Complete the Ukrainian flag.

Serbia

When Serbia and Montenegro separated in 2006, Serbia chose to use red, white, and blue on their flag. The official flag also uses the coat of arms: A double-headed eagle and a cross.

MISSING PIECES

Can you put the puzzle pieces back in the right places?

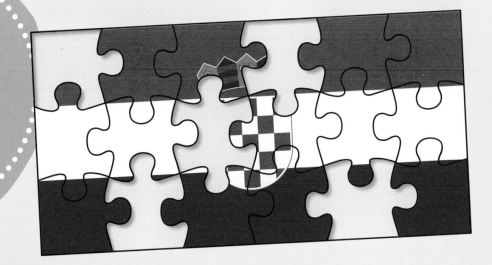

A   B   C   D   E

LOOK CLOSELY!

Can you spot five differences between the correct Slovenian flag below, and the one on the right? Circle each difference.

Shade in a flag each time you find a difference

TWO HALVES

Half of each flag is missing. Can you complete them?

WHICH ONE?

Match each flag to each nation's cyclist. Then guess the country!

Russia

The Russian flag was first used by Peter the Great on Russian ships. His design was inspired by the *tricolores* used in Europe.

Many countries in Europe have used the Russian flag as inspiration for their own. The combination of red, white, and blue is often called "Pan-Slavic." Slavic refers to countries in central and eastern Europe.

North Macedonia

The flag of North Macedonia has been used since 1995. It shows a radiant yellow sun on a red background. Radiant means "sending out light."

Latvia

The Latvian flag dates back to the 13th century. A red flag with a white stripe is spoken of in a medieval document. Today, the red is said to represent the willingness of Latvians to defend their country.

Estonia

The Estonian flag was designed by students in 1881 who were protesting against Russian rule. It has been officially used since Estonia became independent in 1990.

In the Estonian flag, blue represents the sky and loyalty; black is for past suffering and the soil; white is for snow and the struggle for freedom.

Copy the North Macedonian flag!

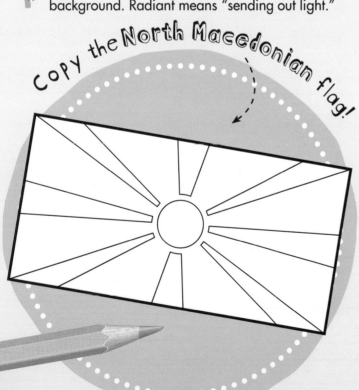

Complete Russia's flag!

Belarus

The Belarusian flag has a pattern of woven cloth along one edge. This cloth represents part of the national costume. The larger red stripe represents struggle and victory, green represents hope.

Bulgaria

Bulgaria was part of the vast Ottoman Empire until 1908. When they became independent, Bulgaria chose a *tricolore* flag using white for peace, green for freedom, and red for the bravery of its people.

Greece

The Greek flag shows nine horizontal blue and white stripes. Blue represents the sky. The cross in the top left corner represents the Greek Christian faith.

Albania

Albania is known as the "land of the eagle." The black eagle has been the Albanian emblem since the 15th century.

Lithuania

The red stripe in the Lithuanian flag comes from the coat of arms, which shows a white knight on a red background. Red also symbolizes courage, green is for hope, and yellow is for plenty.

Complete the emblem.

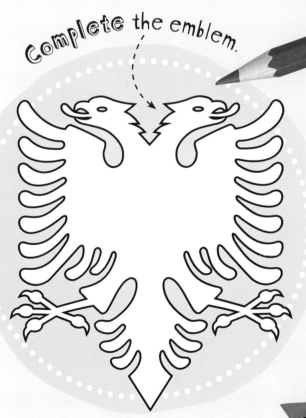

Cyprus

A copper picture of the island appears on Cyprus's flag. Copper was chosen because of the large copper deposits on the island. Beneath the picture of Cyprus are two olive branches to signify peace.

SO MANY STRIPES!

Here are the flags of Russia, Latvia, Estonia, Lithuania, and Belarus. Can you choose the correct artist's palette for each flag?

ESTONIA

LITHUANIA

RUSSIA

BELARUS

Can you complete the flags?

LATVIA

1 2 3 4 5

MAKE A MATCH

Can you match the pairs of flags? Which country's flag is left on its own?

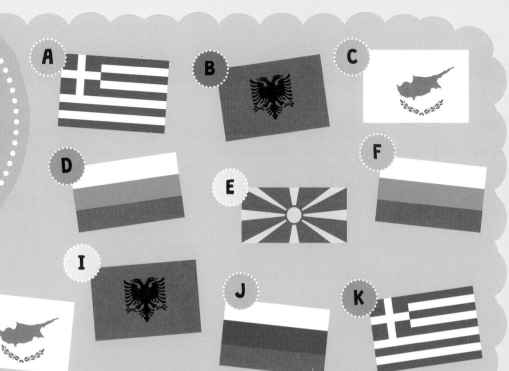

GET IT RIGHT!

Which of these is the correct Greek flag?

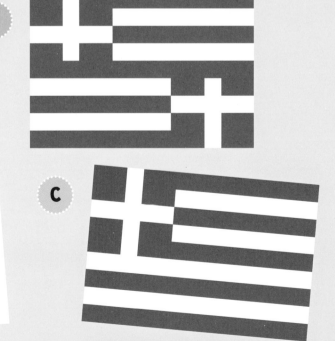

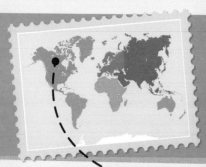
Canada

The big red maple leaf on the Canadian flag is easy to spot! Canada is famous for its many maple trees and maple syrup.

The white of the flag represents the snowy Canadian north, the red is a tribute to the many who fought in the world wars.

Complete Canada's flag.

The provinces

Canada is divided into 13 provinces and territories. Each one has its own flag. Here are some of them:

Northwest Territories

There are 11 languages spoken in the Northwest Territories! Their flag was chosen from competition entries.

Ontario

Ottawa, Canada's capital city, is in the province of Ontario. The flag shows the Union Jack, a symbol of Canada's links with the United Kingdom.

Nova Scotia

St. Andrew's cross appears on Nova Scotia's flag, but with the blue and white reversed. Nova Scotia means "New Scotland." In the middle of the flag are the Scottish Royal Arms.

Nunavut

The majority of the population in Nunavut are Inuit people. They have lived in this region for thousands of years. The flag shows a monument used to mark sacred places.

United States of America

The USA was once part of the British Empire. It declared independence on 4 July 1776. The colonies that originally stood against British rule are remembered in the 13 red and white stripes on the flag.

The stars in the top left corner represent the 50 states of the USA.

Try your own stars and stripes.

State flags

Each of the USA's 50 states have their own flag. Here are some of them:

Arizona

The red and yellow in the Arizona flag stands for the time that Arizona was ruled by Spain. The state has rich mineral deposits, these are represented by the copper star.

California

A grizzly bear strides across the California flag. Above its head is a red star that represents freedom.

Virginia

The round seal on of the Virginia flag shows the figure of Liberty triumphing over Tyranny.

Ohio

The shape of the Ohio flag is called a pennant. It comes from a Civil War cavalry flag. The 17 stars represent the fact that Ohio was the 17th state to join the union that became the United States.

New York

The flag of New York shows two figures: Liberty and justice. The figure of justice wears a blindfold. This symbolizes that everyone is treated equally under the law.

ON THE RAILS

The Canadian Pacific Railway crosses Canada. Can you help it find the right route?

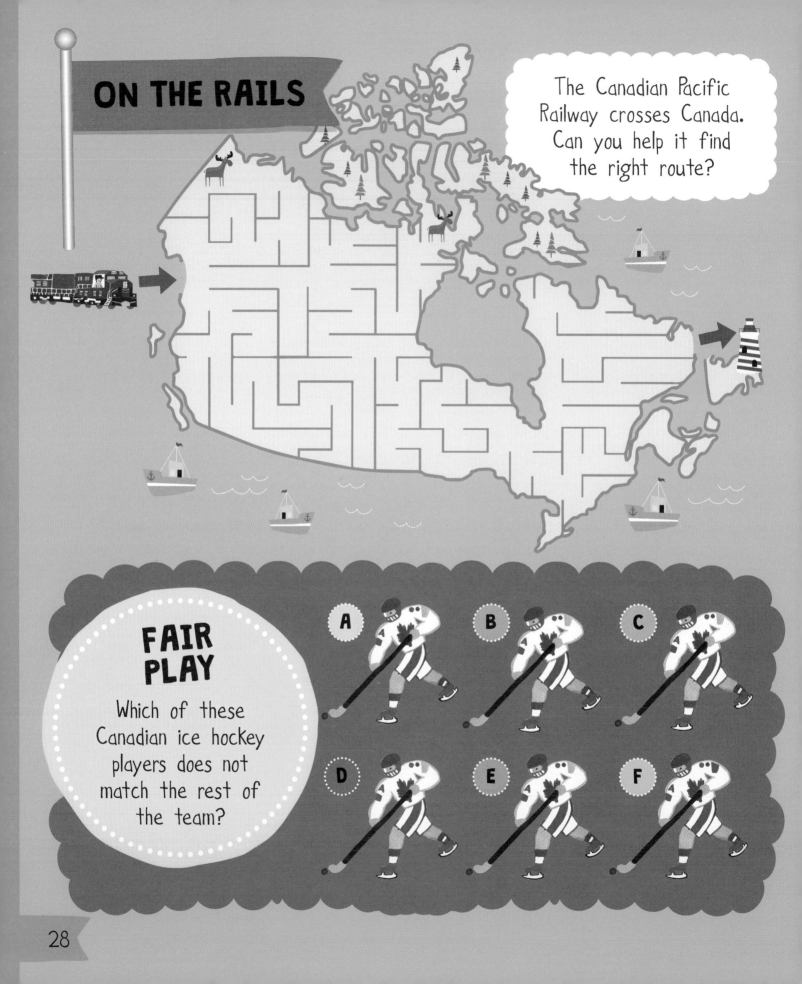

FAIR PLAY

Which of these Canadian ice hockey players does not match the rest of the team?

TOOT! TOOT!

Can you find your way to the American stars and stripes?

LADY LIBERTY

What is missing from each state flag?

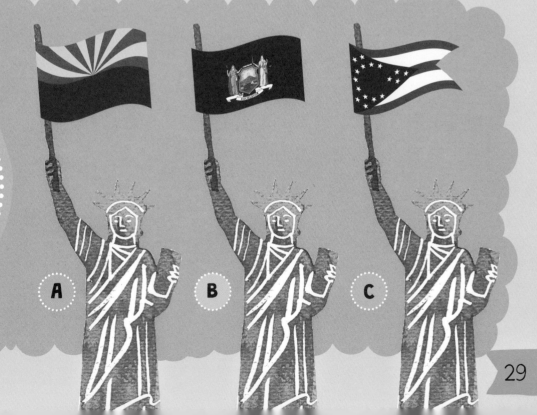

A   B   C

Mexico

The Mexican flag is the same as the flag of Italy, but with the arms of Mexico in the middle. The flag was inspired by the French *tricolore* but in the green, white, and red of the Mexican liberation army.

The symbol of Mexico comes from an Aztec legend. An ancient leader was told by a god to settle where they found an eagle eating a snake, sitting on a cactus. That settlement is now Mexico City!

Complete the Mexican flag

Honduras

In 1823, five Spanish colonies joined together to form the United Provinces of Central America. The five stars on the Honduras flag represent the five colonies.

Complete the Honduran flag

Guatemala

Guatemala's flag features the country's coat of arms. Sitting on a scroll is a red and green quetzal bird—a symbol of liberty.

Belize

The blue and red of the Belize flag stand for the People's United Party. They came to power in 1950 and introduced the flag.

The central emblem shows tools and a mahogany tree to represent the country's logging industry.

Nicaragua

The flag of Nicaragua is similar to that of El Salvador, but the two blues are different. The coat of arms shows a rainbow and the sun's rays to represent a bright future.

Costa Rica

The flag of Costa Rica shares the blue and white of the United Provinces flag, but a red stripe has been added to echo the French *Tricolore*.

Complete the Nicaraguan flag.

Panama

When the Panama flag was designed, the themes of the two main political parties were chosen: Blue for the Conservatives and red for the Liberals. White was chosen to represent peace between them.

The flag of Panama was introduced in 1903 when Panama became an independent nation. It was separated from Colombia so that the Panama Canal could be built.

Complete Panama's flag.

El Salvador

The flag of El Salvador show's the country's national coat of arms in the middle. The white stripe represents the land, as well as peace and prosperity. The blue stripes represent the Caribbean Sea and Pacific Ocean.

AZTEC EAGLE

Which Mexican coat of arms is correct?

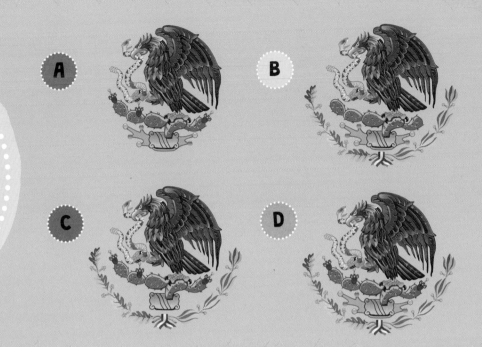

The flags are out! Can you complete the blank flags on each row of bunting?

FLYING THE FLAGS

MIX AND MATCH

Match each flag to its missing design. Then name the country!

A

B

C

D

1

2

3

4

ALL AT SEA

Can you unscramble the letters for each country's boat?

A

RAVALSELOD

B

TOASC ARIC

C

CAIANRUAG

D

MAPNAA

Cuba

Cuba gained independence in 1902. The five stripes stand for the five Cuban provinces at the time of independence, and the triangle for equality.

The star on the flag is called the Lone Star, or *La Estrella Solitaria*. It was inspired by the flag of Texas, which is Known as the Lone Star State.

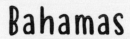

Bahamas

Sea and sand are reflected in the blue and yellow of this island nation's flag. It was a pirate base before it became a British colony in 1783. Bahamas gained independence in 1973.

Ships that are registered in the Bahamas fly the civil ensign. This is the British Red Ensign with a Bahamas flag in the top corner.

Complete the Cuban flag.

Jamaica

The Jamaican flag was chosen from competition entries sent in by the public. The local saying for the flag goes: "Hardships there are but the land is green and the sun shineth."

Complete the Jamaican flag.

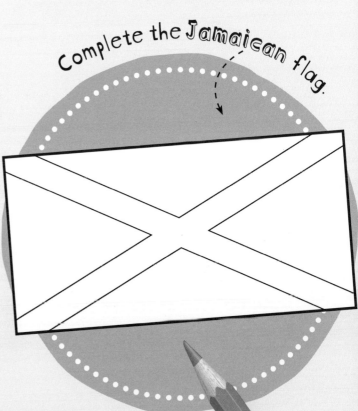

Haiti

The story of the Haitian flag says that during the struggle for independence from French rule, a rebel tore up the French *Tricolore*. The blue and red stripes were stitched back together to create a new flag.

The Arms of Haiti are sometimes used on the flag. The many weapons symbolize their fight for freedom.

Complete the Haitian emblem.

Antigua and Barbuda

The flag of Antigua and Barbuda was chosen from 600 competition entries. The V shape represents victory in independence, and the rising sun stands for a new era.

Complete Antigua and Barbuda's flag.

Dominican Republic

The Dominican Republic flag shares the red and blue of the Haitian flag. Haiti once occupied the Dominican Republic and a new flag was designed by the movement for independence.

Saint Kitts and Nevis

This flag was designed by a student. Red stands for the struggle for freedom; green for fertile land; two stars for hope and liberty; yellow for the sunny climate; and black for Saint Kitts' African ancestry.

THROUGH THE MAZE

Can you find your way to the Bahamas? Mind the sharks!

Can you remember the Jamaican and Cuban flags? Complete these flags without turning back to check!

MAKING MEMORIES

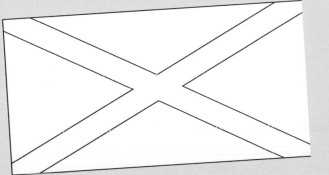

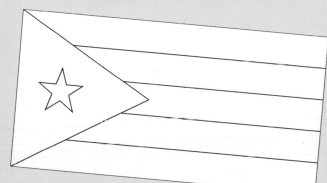

GRID-LOCK

Can you find three flags in the same order as shown below?

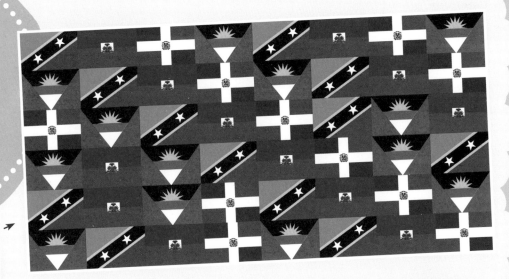

THAT'S TORN IT

Can you put the Antiguan and Barbudan flag back together?

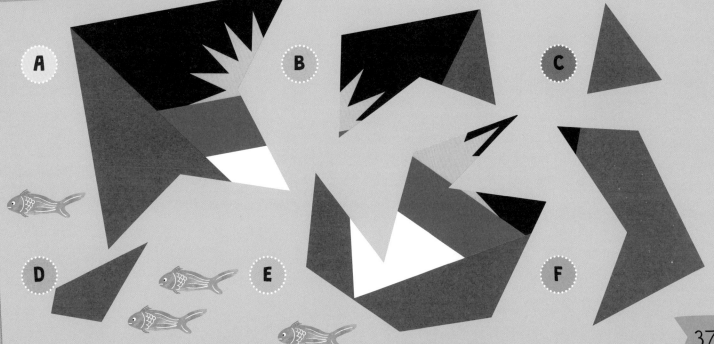

A   B   C

D   E   F

Dominica

In the middle of the Dominica flag is the sisserou parrot. It is an endangered species unique to Dominica. The stars represent the island's ten parishes.

Complete the Dominican flag.

Saint Vincent and the Grenadines

Known locally as the "Gems of the Antilles" the islands of Saint Vincent and the Grenadines gained independence together in 1979. The "gems" in the middle of the flag are arranged into a V shape for Saint Vincent.

Blue represents the clear skies; yellow the sunshine; and green for the island's plants and trees.

Complete the flag.

Grenada

The small shape on the left of the Grenada flag is a nutmeg. Grenada is known for this spice and is sometimes called the "spice island."

The central star stands for the island's capital, St. George's, and the six outer stars for the island's parishes.

Barbados

The trident on the Barbados flag links to Britannia and the time that Barbados was a British colony. It also links to Neptune—god of the Sea—and shows how important the sea is to this island nation.

 The trident does not have a shaft, or handle. This shows that the link with the colonial past is broken.

Saint Lucia

The triangles on the Saint Lucia flag represent two volcanic peaks on the island called the Pitons. The blue represents the Atlantic Ocean, yellow is for sunshine. The black and white represent the country's people.

Trinidad and Tobago

Many designs for the Trinidad and Tobago flag were sent in by the island's people. The flag that was chosen shows black for the land, red for the sun, and white for the sea.

Complete Barbados' flag.

Complete Saint Lucia's flag.

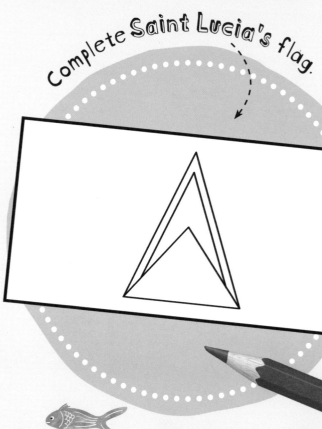

DESTINATION UNKNOWN

Where are each of these adventurers going? Clues on page 38!

A "I'm off to the Pitons!"

B "I'm going to stay in the Gems of the Antilles."

C "I'd like to see a unique parrot."

SUNSHINE SUDOKU

Have a go at the sudoku on the sunny island of Grenada!

		6		3	
3	1	4		2	
		5	1	4	3
1	4	3	2		
	3		5	6	2
	6		3		

PAINT PALETTES

Which flag do you think each of these artists has been painting?

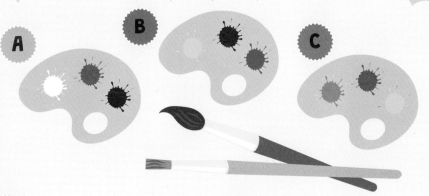

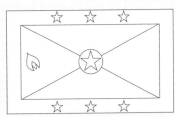

WHAT'S MISSING?

Something is missing from each of these flags. What is it?

ASIA

Turkey

Red has been used on Turkey's flag for centuries. Before becoming a republic, Turkey was part of the great Ottoman Empire. This stretched from North Africa, across Europe to southern Russia!

The crescent and star are symbols of the Islamic religion and so are used by many Muslim countries.

Complete the Turkish flag.

Georgia

Georgia gained independence in 1991. In 2004, its flag was changed to this one, bearing five crosses that stand for the Orthodox Christian faith. It may have been used in the 14th century.

Armenia

Armenia was part of the Ottoman Empire and then became part of the Soviet Union. Armenia gained independence in 1991. In their flag, red stands for the highlands, blue for clear skies, and orange for the crops at harvest.

Azerbaijan

This flag was created when Azerbaijan was briefly independent in 1918, after the fall of the Ottoman Empire. It became the official flag in 1991 when the country became independent again.

Blue stands for the nation, red stands for progress, and green represents Islam.

Lebanon

The tree on the Lebanese flag is the Cedar of Lebanon. It has been a symbol of the country for around 3,000 years.

Iraq

The 2008 flag of Iraq uses the pan-Arab combination of red, white, and black. In the central band is writing in Arabic script, meaning "God is Great."

Israel

The state of Israel was declared independent in 1948. The six-pointed star is a traditional symbol of Judaism. The blue and white stripes are said to be taken from the Jewish prayer shawl.

Tajikistan

The white in the Tajikistan flag represents the country's cotton industry. The central emblem is made of a crown and seven stars.

Complete the Israeli flag.

Uzbekistan

The moon on Uzbekistan's flag stands for the new nation, as it gained independence in 1991. The 12 stars are for the months of the year.

Kazakhstan

The bright blue of the Kazakhstan flag contrasts with yellow of the sun. Beneath the sun is an eagle called a "berkut."

Syria

Syria and Egypt joined to form the United Arab Republic in 1958. The union collapsed in 1961. Syria changed their flag, but returned to this one in 1963.

Kyrgyzstan

Red stands for the country's national hero Manas the Noble who united forty Kyrgyz tribes.

SPOT ON!

Each of these bubbles shows part of a flag. Which countries do the flags belong to?

A

B

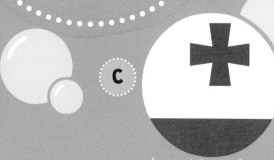

C

D

HERE'S A CLUE

Look at the clues for each person, can you tell which countries they are from?

A

B

C

D

Clues on page 42!

ALL THE ELEMENTS

Can you link the correct missing elements to each flag?

A   B   C   D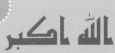

1    2    3    4

IS IT RIGHT?

Which is the correct version of the Kazakhstani flag?

A

B

C

Jordan

Jordan gained independence in 1946. At independence, they added the seven-pointed star to the pan-Arab flag they had already been using.

The seven points on the star represent the verses that open the Quran—the holy book of the Muslim faith.

Complete Jordan's flag.

Saudi Arabia

The green in flag of Saudi Arabia represents the Islamic faith. The writing in the middle is the Muslim Statement of Faith. The sword represents one given to King Abd-al Aziz who unified the kingdom in 1932.

Kuwait

The shape at the left of the Kuwaiti flag is a trapezium. In the flag, red stands for bloodshed, white for purity, green for fertility, and black for the defeat of the enemy.

Bahrain

Bahrain is a group of islands linked to Saudi Arabia by a 25-km (15-mile) causeway. The white stripe was added to the flag in 1820 to show that their ships were not pirates.

Qatar

The dark red of Qatar's flag is known as "Qatar Maroon." It is said that the shade comes from the way dye in the original red cloth changed in the sun.

United Arab Emirates

The seven states of the United Arab Emirates came together in 1971. The red section stands for the tradition of emirates flags being red. The black in the flag stands for the oil wealth of the region.

Yemen

The current Yemen flag was created when two nations joined together to form one state. Red, white, and black were shared elements between the two nations' flags.

Complete the Yemeni flag.

Iran

Green, white, and red have been used by Iran for centuries. Where the stripes meet, writing from the Quran has been made into an emblem. It means "God is Great."

Turkmenistan

Originally part of Russia, Turkmenistan became independent in 1991. The strip at the left side shows five traditional carpet designs and a wreath of olive leaves.

Afghanistan

Due to unrest and changes in the country, Afghanistan has changed its flag more times than any other country. Most versions have used black, red, and green. The current coat of arms stands in the middle.

Oman

The use of red in flags is traditional in this region. The white stands for peace and the green for the country's mountains. The emblem of swords and a curved dagger stands for the ruling dynasty.

Pakistan

In 1947, Pakistan separated from India to form a separate state. Green in the flag represents Muslims, and the white strip the non-Muslim population. The star stands for light and knowledge, the crescent for progress.

CAMEL RACES

Which camel will get to the camp first?

LET'S REPAIR

These flags have been damaged. Can you find the missing piece for each one?

1 Bahrain

2 United Arab Emirates

3 Jordan

 A

 B

 C

 D

 E

 F

SORT IT OUT

These flags have been sewn together wrong. Can you work out the right order for the pieces?

 A

 B

C

A

B

C

QUICK QUIZ!

How much can you remember about the flags on pages 46–47?

1. What do many flags in the Arab region have in common?

2. Which country's flag shows a star for light and knowledge?

3. What does the unusual panel on the Turkmenistan flag show?

4. What does green stand for in Oman's flag?

5. Complete this flag without turning back? Which country's flag is it?

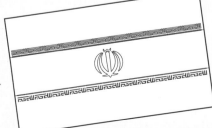

49

India

This flag has been used since India gained independence from British rule in 1947.

Orange or saffron stands for courage and sacrifice, white for purity and truth, and green for faith and fertility.

The wheel emblem is called the "chakra" and represents the movement of life.

Complete the Indian flag.

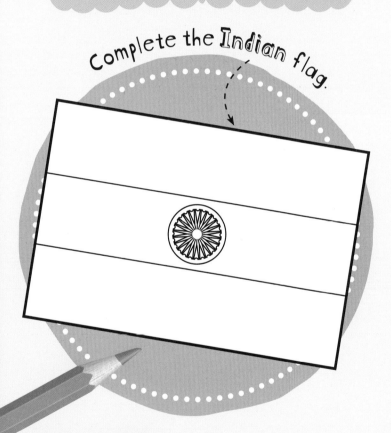

Nepal

The shape of the Nepalese flag is unique. It shows a crescent moon and a sun in two triangles. Red represents the rhododendron, the country's national flower, blue stands for peace.

Bhutan

In the local language, Bhutan means "land of the dragon." The dragon that stands on the flag is white, symbolizing purity. Orange stands for the country's Buddhist religion and yellow for the ruling family.

Sri Lanka

The island of Sri Lanka was known Ceylon until 1972.

Three religions are represented on the flag: green for Muslims, orange for Hindus, yellow for Buddhists.

The lion is the symbol of Sri Lanka. The island's name comes from the word "Sinhala," which means lion.

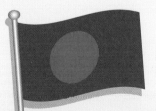

Bangladesh

The green of the Bangladeshi flag represents the land and red stands for the struggle for freedom. This flag was first used when Bangladesh gained independence in 1971.

Maldives

The Maldives are a string of small islands in the Indian Ocean. They became independent in 1965 and their new flag was introduced. Red comes from their original flag, green is for Islam and peace.

China

China was established as a communist republic in 1949. Red is traditional for the Chinese people and it also symbolizes revolution. The big star represents the Communist Party and the smaller stars stand for the country's social classes.

Complete the Chinese flag.

Myanmar

Myanmar was known as Burma until the name was changed by the ruling military in 1989. The flag was changed in 2010. This flag is similar to one used in the country during Japanese occupation in 1943–1945.

Laos

Laos gained independence in 1953 and has been under communist rule since 1975. The blue stripe in the middle shows the full moon over the Mekong River.

Thailand

Thailand's flag was originally red with a white elephant in the middle. The stripes of white and blue were added to express support for European nations during World War I.

Mongolia

The emblem at the left of the Mongolian flag is the Soyonbo, it combines many symbols of Buddhism. The red was originally used in the flag of revolution and todays stands for progress.

Vietnam

Vietnam was part of a French colony called Indochina. It was invaded by Japan during World War II. The country was divided into two, then was reunited following the Vietnam War in 1976.

Red stands for bloodshed and the five-pointed star for the country's workers.

READY TO PLAY

These cricketers are ready for a tournament. Can you work out which country each one plays for?

Clues on page 50

A B C D E

ON THE MOUNTAIN

These hikers are trying to find their way to the Himalaya Mountains in Nepal, can you help them?

LOST PANDA

The Chinese panda needs to find its way home to the bamboo forest. Can you help?

WHICH ONE?

Which are the correct Thai and Mongolian flags?

THAILAND

 A

B

C

MONGOLIA

A

B

C

Cambodia

Having been under both French and Japanese rule, Cambodia became independent in 1953. In 1993 the Cambodian monarchy was restored to power. This flag is from 1948 but was re-introduced in 1993.

The ancient temple of Angkor Wat is shown on the flag.

Malaysia

The flag of Malaysia is based on the USA's design. The crescent and star stand for Islam. There are eleven stripes and eleven points on the star, these stand for the eleven states that make up the nation.

Singapore

Singapore means "lion city." This city became a trading post for the British empire in 1819. It joined Malaysia in 1963 then became independent in 1965.

Singapore's five stars represent democracy, peace, equality, justice, and peace.

Indonesia

The Indonesian flag is based on one used in the region in the 13th century. Red stands for the body and white for the soul or spirit. The country gained independence from Dutch rule in 1949.

Complete the Indonesian flag.

Timor-Leste

The flag of Timor-Leste was designed in 1975 but not used until independence in 2002. Red stands for bloodshed in the fight for independence. Black stands for oppression, yellow for hope, and the white star for peace.

Japan

A bright red sun sits in the middle of a white field. The sun has been a symbol of Japan for thousands of years. The red disc is called *Hinomaru*, or Lucky Sun.

Complete the Japanese flag.

The Korean peninsula was divided into North and South territories in 1948.

North Korea

The flag of North Korea shows a red star for communism, along with the country's traditional red, white, and blue.

South Korea

South Korea uses the traditional Korean red, white, and blue. The symbol in the middle is called yin-yang and represents harmony of opposites.

The shapes around the South Korean flag are called trigrams or *Kwae*. They represent heaven, water, earth, and fire.

Philippines

The Philippines was ruled by Spain, and then the USA. They gained independence in 1949. Red stands for bravery, white for peace, and blue for loyalty to country.

The eight rays of the sun on the Philippines' flag stand for the eight provinces that stood against Spanish rule.

Brunei

Brunei is a monarchy, ruled by a Sultan. The yellow of the flag stands for the Sultan, the stripes for his ministers. The coat of arms has five elements, including the crescent of Islam.

AT THE TEMPLE

Can you circle five differences between these two Cambodian temples?

Shade in a flag each time you find a difference.

Complete the Malaysian flag by putting the puzzle pieces back in the right places.

IT'S A PUZZLE

A
B
C
D
E

IN A ROW

Can you find three flags in the same order as shown below?

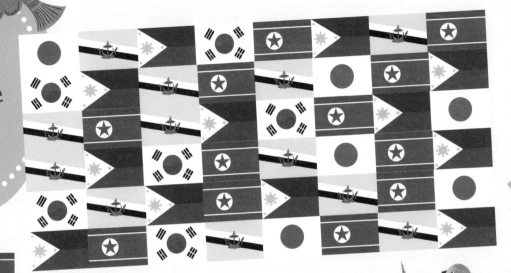

LET'S CLIMB

It's time for a hike in Japan. Which trail leads to the top of Mount Fuji?

A

B

C

AFRICA

Morocco

The bright red of the Morocco flag has been used for centuries. The five points of the star represent the five main rules of the Muslim faith.

Algeria

Algeria was a French colony until 1962 when they became independent. Their flag was designed by the National Liberation Front who led the movement for independence.

Tunisia

The crescent and star on the Turkish flag are symbols of Islam. The crescent has also been used in North Africa for a long time.

Libya

Libya's flag was reintroduced in 2011 having first been used in 1951. The three stripes stand for the country's main regions. The crescent and star stand for Islam.

Egypt

The flag of Egypt uses the Pan-Arab stripes. On the middle white stripe is the Eagle of Saladin. Saladin was a famous ruler in the 12th century.

Sudan

Sudan shares the Pan-Arab red, white, and black with many other countries. The green triangle represents both Islam and prosperity. This flag was chosen from competition entries in 1968.

Eritrea

Eritrea was once joined with Ethiopia, but gained independence in 1993. The emblem shows an olive branch.

Cabo Verde

In 2013, Cape Verde changed its name to The Republic of Cabo Verde. The stripes across the flag represent the road to independence from Portuguese rule.

Mauritania

Mauritania's full name is The Mauritanian Islamic Republic. The green of the flag and the crescent stand for the country's Muslim faith.

Mali

Mali was a French colony until 1960. The flag is inspired by the French *tricolore*. Green stands for nature, yellow for mineral wealth, and red for struggle and sacrifice.

Senegal

Senegal and Mali achieved independence from France as a united federation. They separated later the same year, but their flags remain similar.

The five-pointed star is called a pentagram. It is known as the "Seal of Solomon" and was added in 1915.

The Gambia

The River Gambia flows through this country, the smallest on the African continent. In the flag, red represents the savannah earth, green the forest, and blue the river running through it.

Complete the Egyptian flag!

Guinea-Bissau

This flag has been used since Guinea-Bissau became independent in 1973. Bissau is the country's capital city, it was added to the country name to make it different from Guinea.

Guinea

Guinea was known as "French Guinea" until independence in 1958. The Pan-African *tricolore* was taken from the movement for independence.

PYRAMID PUZZLE

These visitors are off to the Egyptian pyramids. Help them get there!

Can you fill in the blank flags to complete the patterns?

BIRTHDAY BUNTING

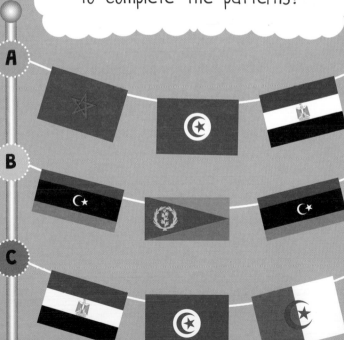

A

B

C

SNIP! SNIP!

These flags have been snipped up! Match the right pieces back together, and then name them.

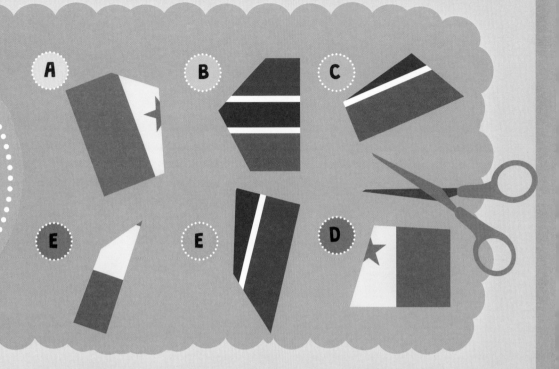

A B C
E E D

IN A MUDDLE

Each of these flags is missing an important piece. Can you find the right one for each flag?

1 Cabo Verde
2 Mauritania
3 Guinea-Bissau

A
B
C
D
E
F

Niger

The flag of Niger is similar to the Côte D'Ivoire because they were designed at the same time. The two countries formed an alliance with Chad and Benin, and later achieved independence.

The yellow of the flag symbolizes the hot Sahara regions, green is for the forest, white is for the River Niger, and the yellow circle is for the sun.

Djibouti

Djibouti was originally called the Territory of the Afars and Issars—the two main ethnic groups of the country. Blue stands for the Issars, green for the Afars, and the star and white for unity and peace.

Chad

Chad was once a French province and became independent in 1960. Their flag combines the French *Tricolore* with the Pan-African combination.

Chad's flag is accidentally the same as Romania's!

Somalia

Somalia has a troubled history. In 1960 British and Italian Somaliland united to form Somalia. For a time, the state was controlled by the UN. The blue in the flag is called "UN blue."

The star is said to stand for five branches of Somali people.

Central African Republic

The star at the top of this flag stands for a bright future. It was designed when leaders hoped to unite many countries in a French federation. The flag combines the French *tricolore* and the Pan-African combination.

Ethiopia

The emblem of Ethiopia stands for unity and diversity. The green, yellow, and red stripes were first used on a flag in 1895.

South Sudan

South Sudan is a young nation that gained independence in 2011 when it separated form Sudan. The blue represents the River Nile and the star represents the states of the country.

Sierra Leone

Sierra Leone was founded in 1787 as a home for freed slaves. In 1808 it became a British colony and then gained independence in 1961.

Blue stands for the country's coastal capital, Freetown.

Liberia

Liberia was also established as a home for freed slaves. It was founded by the American Colonization Society in 1816. The flag recalls the USA's stars and stripes design.

Côte D'Ivoire

The Côte D'Ivoire shares history with Niger. Both countries achieved independence together in 1960. Their flags were designed at the same time.

Burkina Faso

Burkina Faso uses the Pan-African combination: Green represents natural resources, red is for revolution, and the yellow star is for the guiding light of the revolution.

Togo

During World War I the German colony of Togo was divided between France and Britain. The French part became independent as Togo in 1960, and the British part became part of Ghana.

Ghana

European nations colonized much of Africa in the 19th century. Ghana became independent in 1957, the first of the British colonies to do so. The flag was inspired by Ethiopia's, an older independent nation.

The Ghanaian flag inspired the use of red, yellow, green, and black across Africa.

Complete Ghana's flag.

LET'S PAINT!

Can you remember how to complete these flags?

A

Central African Republic

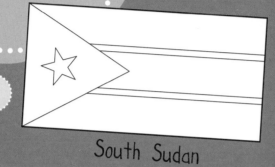

B

South Sudan

C

Djibouti

These cars are having a race! Can you work out who is winning? The car with the highest score is out in front.

LET'S RACE!

4+5+6+7=

5+3+7+2=

9+2+5+1=

7+2+9+1=

HUBBLE, BUBBLE!

Can you guess which flags these bubbles come from?

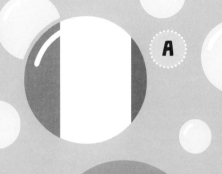

A

B

C

D

Clues on page 63

FLAG FLYING

Which flag should each of the boats be flying?

A

Liberia

B

Ghana

D

Sierra Leone

C

Burkina Faso

1

2

3

4

Benin

Benin was known as Dahomey until 1975. This flag was first used at independence in 1960, but was changed in 1975. It was re-introduced in 1990.

Nigeria

Nigeria became Britain's largest West African colony before gaining independence in 1960. Its flag was chosen from thousands sent in for a public competition.

Cameroon

Cameroon was a German colony and was split between British and French control after World War I. French Cameroon became independent in 1960 and adopted a *tricolore* flag but with green, red, and yellow.

The star was added to the flag in 1961 when British Cameroon joined French Cameroon.

Gabon

Much of this west African nation is covered with rainforest. The green and yellow stripes in the flag represent its rich natural resources. Blue represents the sea.

Equatorial Guinea

This former Spanish colony gained independence in 1968. It is made up of five islands and one mainland state.

The coat of arms shows a silk-cotton tree and six stars to represent the island's states.

São Tomé and Príncipe

These two islands became independent in 1975. The two stars on the central yellow stripe represent the islands, and the red triangle stands for the struggle for independence.

Complete São Tomé and Príncipe's flag.

Congo

Congo's flag shares green, yellow, and red with many other African nations but the diagonal design is unique. Congo was a French colony until independence in 1960.

Uganda

The great crested crane is Uganda's national bird and appears on a badge in the middle of the flag. The stripes represent the people, sunlight, and brotherhood.

Democratic Republic of the Congo

The flag of the Democratic Republic of the Congo has changed many times. This design has been used since 2006. Blue stands for peace, red for past sacrifice, and yellow for prosperity.

The star stands for unity and a bright future.

Complete the Ugandan flag.

Angola

The flag of Angola uses a half-cogwheel and machete to create a similar symbol to the hammer and sickle on the old Soviet flag. The cogwheel stands for industry and the machete for agriculture.

Kenya

In the middle of the Kenyan flag is a Maasai shield and spears. The Maasai are an ethnic group who live off the land in Kenya and Tanzania.

Rwanda

Rwanda has a troubled past with fighting between ethnic groups; the Hutus and Tutsis. In 2001, this flag was introduced. It is designed to symbolize unity, peace, and hope for the future.

Burundi

Burundi became an independent kingdom in 1962, and a republic in 1966. The stars on the flag represent the country's three ethnic groups: Hutu, Tutsi, and Twa.

It's competition time! Can you match the player to the right flag for each team?

A B C D

1 2 3 4

MIX-UP!

Half of each flag is missing. Can you complete them?

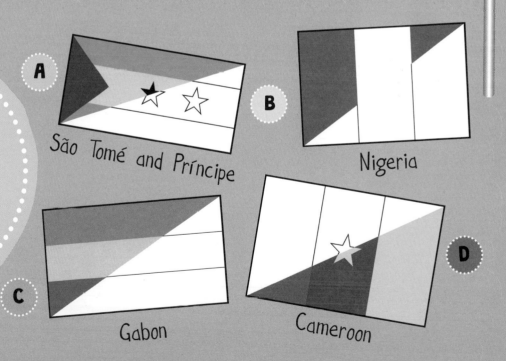

A — São Tomé and Príncipe

B — Nigeria

C — Gabon

D — Cameroon

OSTRICH RACE

These ostriches are racing to the waterhole. Who is going to get there first?

SNAP! SNAP!

Some visitors have taken photos of their trip, but they have missed parts of the flags off. Which countries have they been to?

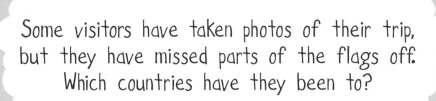

A

B

C

D

E

F

Tanzania

In 1964, the Republic of Zanzibar united with the former British colony of Tanganyika to form Tanzania. The flag uses elements from both countries' original flags.

Green and black represent the land and people, blue is for the sea, and yellow for wealth.

Malawi

The rising sun on Malawi's flag is called the "kwacha." It symbolizes hope and a new dawn for Africa.

Complete Malawi's flag.

Seychelles

The island nation of the Seychelles became independent in 1976. This flag has been used since 1996. The stripes stand for political parties, as well as a bright future.

Comoros

The four stripes and stars of the Comoros flag represent the four islands that make up the nation. The crescent and green are symbolic of Islam.

Madagascar

Red and white on the Madagascan flag stand for the Merina Kingdom, who ruled over the island until 1896. Green stands for the Hova, the country's agricultural workers.

Mauritius

This bright flag has been used since Mauritius became independent in 1968. Red stands for independence, blue for the ocean, yellow for a bright future, and green for the island's forests.

Mozambique

The flag of Mozambique has been used since 1983 when the emblem was changed. The star is overlain with a book, rifle, and hoe.

Zambia

The eagle on Zambia's flag is called the "eagle of liberty." It is said to represent the peoples' ability to rise above problems.

Zimbabwe

Before Zimbabwe became independent it was a British colony known as Rhodesia. The emblem is known as the Zimbabwe bird and represents birds found in an ancient city.

Namibia

Namibia became independent in 1990 having been controlled by South Africa. The flag is inspired by the country's political parties. The radiant sun stands for life and energy.

Botswana

Blue in Botswana's flag represents water or rain, which also symbolizes life in a country that often experiences drought. The black and white band stands for harmony of its people.

Eswatini

Eswatini was known as Swaziland until 2018. The country has been ruled as a monarchy since independence from Britain in 1968.

Lesotho

This flag was first used in 2006 to celebrate 40 years of independence for Lesotho. On the new flag, a shield has been replaced with a "mokorotlo"—a Basotho hat. This represents peace in the country.

South Africa

Having suffered from racial divisions, South Africa introduced a democratic multi-racial government in 1994. This flag represents both the country's past and future.

In the flag blue, red, and white recall European flags; while black, green, and yellow are from the African National Congress party. The Y-shape symbolizes past division coming together in unity.

Complete the South African flag.

RAINBOW FLAGS

Without turning back, can you complete the flags of these nations?

A Seychelles

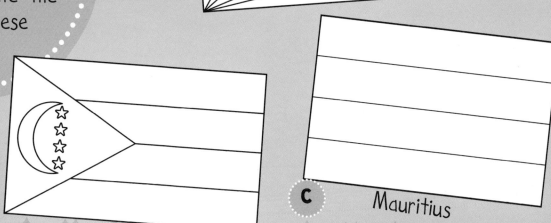

B Comoros

C Mauritius

IMPALA PUZZLE

The impala needs to reach the rest of the herd. Can you help her reach them using the shades only of the Tanzanian flag?

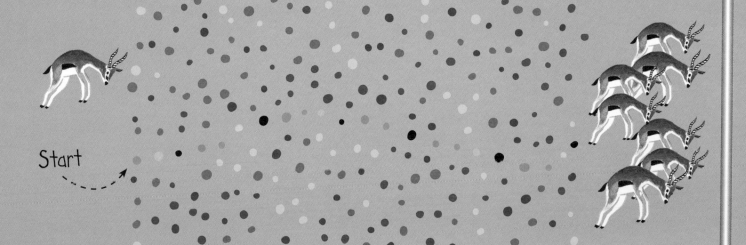

Start

ANIMAL PARADE

Which animal has the correct flag for South Africa?

A

B

C

D

MISSING ELEMENTS

Can you choose the correct elements for these flags?

1

2

3

A

B

C

D

E

F

Colombia, Venezuela, and Ecuador were under Spanish rule until 1819. In 1822 they formed Gran Colombia, then became independent in 1830.

Venezuela

The flag of Venezuela has changed many times. The stars stand for the eight provinces that supported the movement for independence from Spanish rule.

Venezuela's flag sometimes shows the country's coat of arms. in the top left corner.

Colombia

The flag of Colombia shares yellow, blue, and red horizontal stripes with Venezuela and Ecuador. Yellow stands for justice, blue for nobility, and red for courage.

Ecuador

Ecuador's flag is similar to that of Colombia, but the coat of arms stands in the middle. The arms show the River Guayas, a ship, and an Andean condor.

Ecuador takes its name from the Equator, which runs through it.

Complete the Venezuelan flag.

Guyana

The flag of Guyana is known as the "golden arrow." Red stands for the energy of the people, green for the country's forests, white for the rivers, black for endurance, and the golden arrow for a bright future.

Try your own Guyanese flag.

Peru

Peru was an Inca Empire before being taken over by Spanish invaders. They ruled the country until a movement for independence in 1826. Red and white represent the Inca empire.

The coat of arms for Peru shows a llama, a cinchona tree, and a horn of plenty. Palm and laurel leaves symbolize peace.

Here's the Peruvian coat of arms.

Suriname

This flag was chosen from designs sent in by the public. The star is a symbol of unity and hope. The white, green, and red bands stand for justice and freedom.

THE RIGHT STRIPES

Which versions of the Venezuelan and Colombian flags are correct?

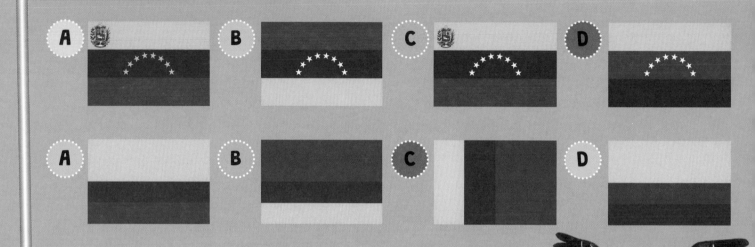

A   B   C   D

A   B   C   D

HAVE A TRY!

Take a look at the coat of arms for Ecuador. Why not try designing one for a school or sports team?

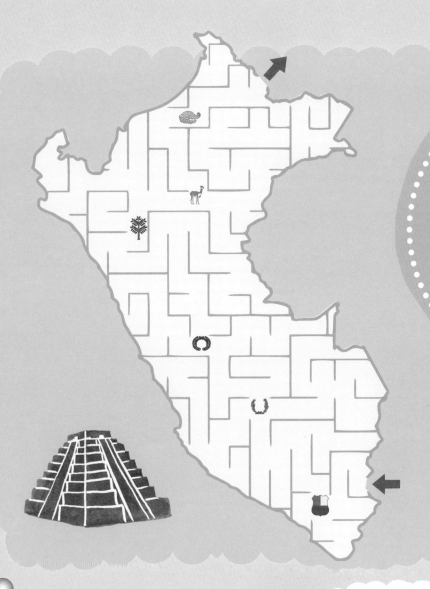

LLAMA LINES

Help the llama cross Peru and collect the elements of the coat of arms on the way!

BITS AND PIECES

Can you put the sections of the Guyanese flag back in the right order?

A   B   C   D   E   F

77

Brazil

The blue disc on Brazil's flag represents the sky as seen on the day it became an independent nation: 15 November 1889. The white band has the motto "order and progress."

The green of the flag represents the vast Amazon rainforest and the yellow the country's mineral wealth.

Complete the Brazilian flag.

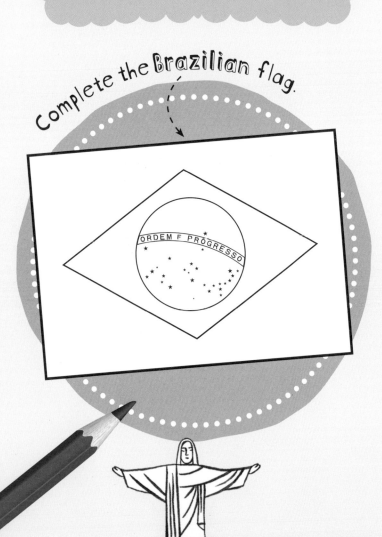

Paraguay

The red, white, and blue stripes of Paraguay's flag represent justice, peace, and liberty. Paraguay has an unusual flag: The reverse shows a different emblem with a lion in the middle.

Complete Paraguay's flag.

Bolivia

Bolivia is named after Simon Bolivar, who liberated many South American countries from Spanish rule. Red stands for courage, yellow for mineral wealth, and green for fertile lands.

The Bolivian coat of arms has lots to show, including a mountain, an alpaca, a wheatsheaf, and a breadfruit tree.

Chile

Spanish explorers established a capital in Chile, Santiago, in 1541. They ruled the country until 1818 when Chileans fought for independence. The flag bears the "lone star" representing progress.

The blue in Chile's flag represents the sky, the white the Andes Mountains with their snow capped peaks, and red for the blood shed in the struggle for independence.

Complete the Chilean flag.

Argentina

The Argentinian flag was designed by a leader in the independence movement. He chose the sky blue and white worn by supporters of independence from Spanish rule. They achieved independence in 1816.

The sun on the flag is known as the Sun of May and was taken from a symbol on Argentinian coins.

Uruguay

Uruguay was a Spanish colony, then passed to Brazilian and then Argentinian control. It became independent in 1830. The blue and white come from the Argentinian flag, and the nine stripes represent the country's nine regions.

Uruguay's flag also shows the Sun of May. Legend states that the sun broke through the clouds the moment that independence was declared!

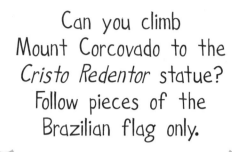

STILL AS A STATUE

Can you climb Mount Corcovado to the *Cristo Redentor* statue? Follow pieces of the Brazilian flag only.

IT'S A PUZZLE

Can you put the Paraguayan puzzle pieces back in the right places?

A

B

C

D

E

MONKEY MISCHIEF

The capuchin monkeys have torn these flags up! Which country's flag is each monkey playing with?

RALLY ROUND!

Can you spot these three flags in this order in the grid below?

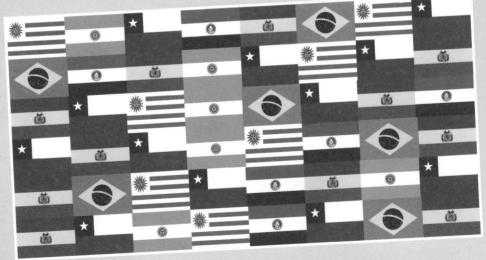

OCEANIA

Australia

The British flag was flown in Australia until 1954. It still appears on the flag. The large seven-pointed star represents the country's seven territories.

The smaller stars on the Australian flag represent the Southern Cross. A constellation in the southern hemisphere.

New Zealand

British explorers arrived in New Zealand in 1769. The islands became British colony in the 1800s. The Union Jack remains on the flag. The stars represent the Southern Cross.

Papua New Guinea

The flag of Papua New Guinea shows a bird of paradise and the Southern Cross. Red and black are used in the country's indigenous artwork.

Complete Papua New Guinea's flag.

Palau

The full moon sits just to the left on the Palau flag. The time of the full moon is said to be the best time for human activity, whether it is celebrating or harvesting!

Blue represents the change from foreign rule to self-government in 1994.

Micronesia

The four islands of Micronesia are each represented as a star on its flag. The islands became independent in 1986. The blue represents the vast Pacific Ocean.

Marshall Islands

The Marshall Islands gained self-governance in 1979. Their new flag was designed by the wife of the president of the new government. The two rays stand for the two strings of islands that make up the nation.

Many of the island nations of the tropical western Pacific Ocean were controlled by the US as the UN Trust Territory of the Pacific Islands from 1947 until 1986.

Try your own Micronesian flag.

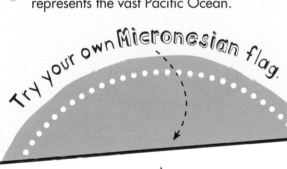

Complete the flag of the Marshall Islands!

AUSSIE TOUR

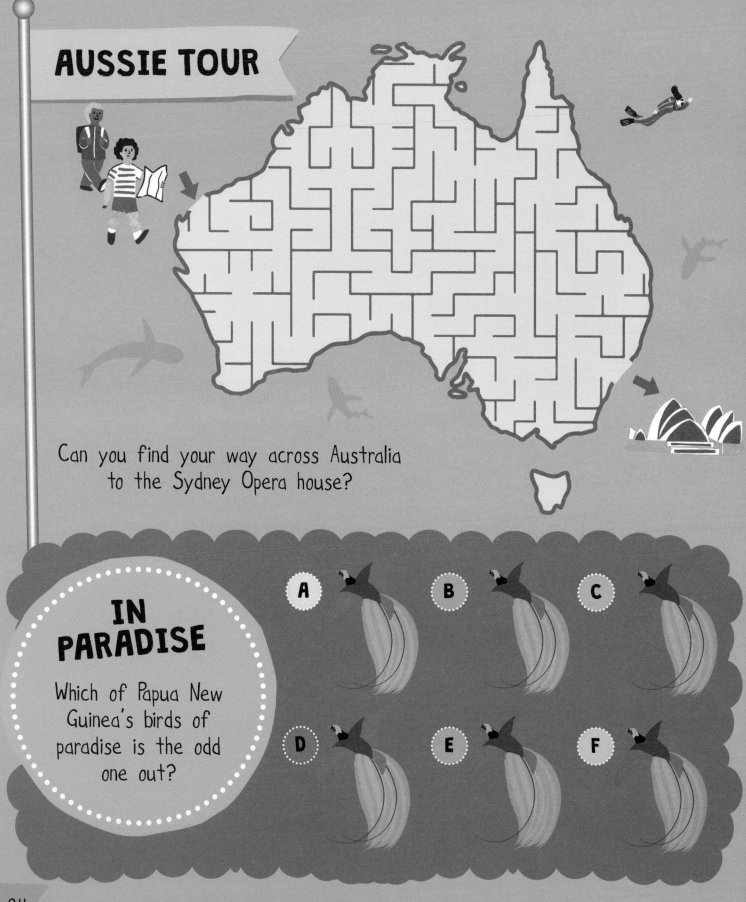

Can you find your way across Australia to the Sydney Opera house?

IN PARADISE

Which of Papua New Guinea's birds of paradise is the odd one out?

A
B
C
D
E
F

ALL CALM

The flags are flying but there isn't any wind! Can you tell which country each one is from?

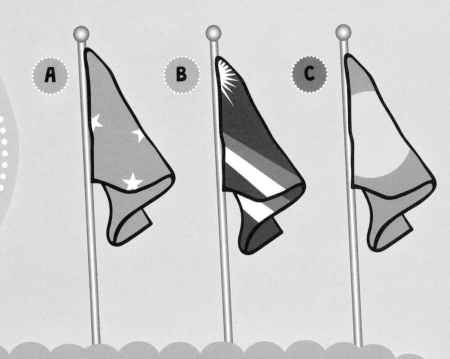

A
B
C

TIME TO SWIM

Help the divers back to their islands! Which country is each diver from?

A
B
C
D

Nauru

The yellow stripe on Nauru's flag represents the equator passing through the blue of the Pacific Ocean. The star's position on the flag represents Nauru's position at one degree south of the equator.

The star has twelve points, which symbolize the twelve tribes that originally lived on the island.

Fiji

The bright blue of the Fijian flag represents the importance of the Pacific Ocean to life on the island. The Union Jack represents the history of the island as it was once a British colony.

The arms of Fiji shows a lion holding a coconut, sugarcane, coconut palms, a dove of peace, and a bunch of bananas.

Complete the Nauruan flag.

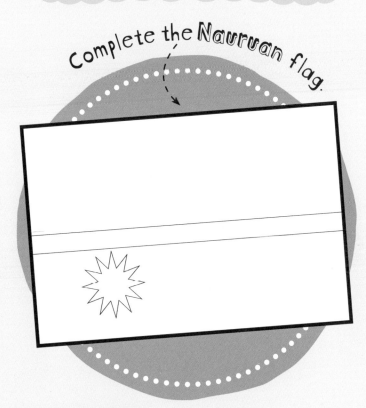

Vanuatu

The emblem on Vanuatu's flag is a curled boar's tusk, inside it are namele fern leaves. These objects represent prosperity and peace. The Y shape in the flag represents the shape of this group of islands.

Complete the Vanuatuan flag.

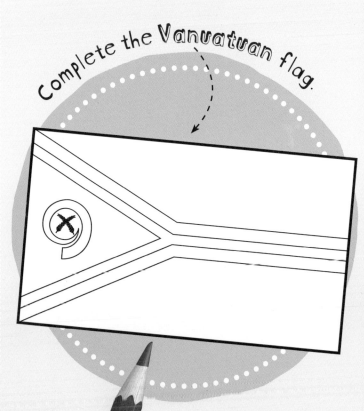

Solomon Islands

Hundreds of islands are grouped together to form the nation of the Solomon Islands. The five stars represent the five main groups. Yellow represents sunshine, blue the sea, and green the land.

Tuvalu

Tuvalu was once part of the island group called the Gilbert and Ellice islands. They became independent in 1978. The nine stars on the flag represent the nine islands that make up the nation—although Tuvalu actually means "eight islands."

Complete the Tuvaluan flag.

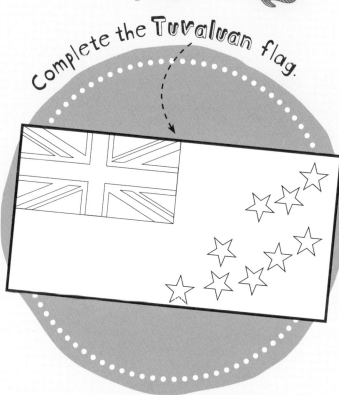

Kiribati

Once known as the "Gilberts," Kiribati became independent in 1979. This flag was hoisted on Kiribati's independence day. The bird is a frigate bird and represents the importance of the sea.

Tonga

This flag has been used since 1862 when Tonga's King George Tupou I introduced it. He wanted a flag that would symbolize the Christian faith. The constitution of 1875 says that the flag must never be altered.

Complete the Tongan flag.

Samoa

This flag was designed in 1948 when Samoa was a territory of New Zealand. Samoa became independent in 1962. White stands for purity, blue for freedom, and red for courage.

SNIP! SNIP!

These flags have been snipped into pieces. Can put them back together?

FILL ME IN

Can you complete the coat of arms of Fiji without turning back?

FLYING HIGH

Which is the correct flag for Kiribati?

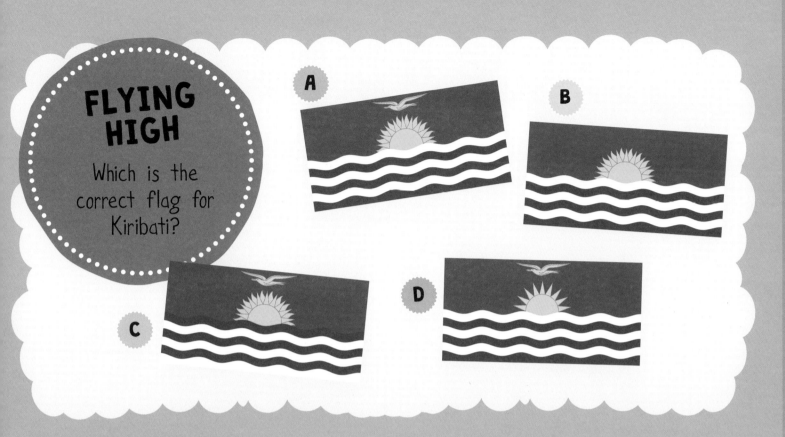

A

B

C

D

ON YOUR MARKS ...

A

B

Help the boats through the islands! Collect the letters as you go, then work out which country each boat belongs to.

n a
g
T o g S
a
a o
a m

ANSWERS

Page 8
Letter land

A Sweden, B Finland, C Iceland,
D Norway, E Denmark

Memory test

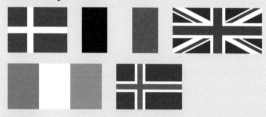

Page 9
Patch it up

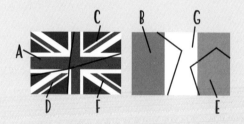

Page 12
Win the race!

A Portugal

Two halves

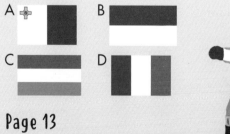

Page 13
Bubble trouble

A Italy, B Malta, C Spain, D Portugal

Quick quiz!

1 Napoleon, 2 the George Cross, 3 Because it was once a great seafaring nation, 4 No other nation was using red and yellow, 5 San Marino.

Page 16
Three to find

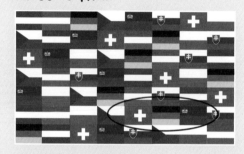

Memory test

A

B

C

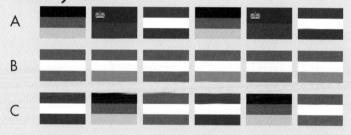

Page 17
Paint the flag

1–C Hungary, 2–A Slovakia, 3–B Poland

Number crunching

4	2	3	5	1	6
5	6	1	3	2	4
1	5	4	2	6	3
2	3	6	4	5	1
3	1	2	6	4	5
6	4	5	1	3	2

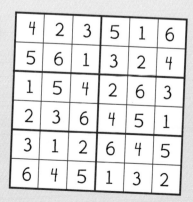

Page 20
Missing pieces

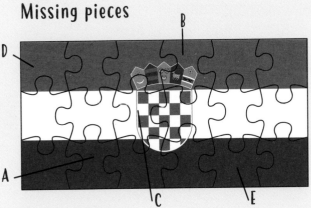

Look closely!

Page 21
Two halves

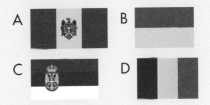

Which one?

A–3 Moldova, B–1 Serbia, C–2 Ukraine

Page 24
So many stripes!

Russia 3, Latvia 2, Estonia 1, Lithuania 5, Belarus 4

Page 25
Make a match

Greece A–K, Albania B–I, Cyprus C–H,
Macedonia D–F, Bulgaria E–G.
Russia is left on its own

Get it right!

C

Page 28
On the rails

Fair play

F

Page 29
Toot! Toot!

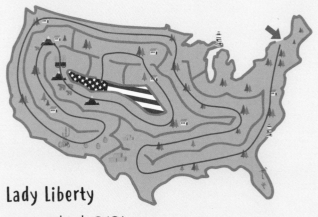

Lady Liberty

A star, B bird, C 'O'

Page 32
Aztec eagle

D

Flying the flags

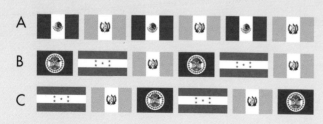

A

B

C

Page 33
Mix and match

A–2 El Salvador, B–4 Nicaragua, C–1 Panama,
D–3 Costa Rica

All at sea

A El Salvador, B Costa Rica, C Nicaragua,
D Panama

Page 36
Through the maze

B

Making memories

Page 37
Grid-lock

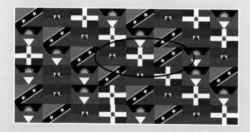

That's torn it

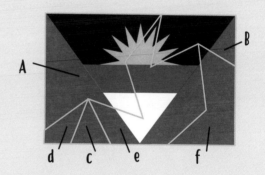

Page 40
Destination unknown

A Saint Lucia, B Saint Vincent and the Grenadines,
C Dominica

Sunshine sudoku

2	5	6	4	3	1
3	1	4	6	2	5
6	2	5	1	4	3
1	4	3	2	5	6
4	3	1	5	6	2
5	6	2	3	1	4

Page 41
Paint palettes

A–3 Trinidad and Tobago, B–1 Barbados,
C–2 Grenada

What's missing?

A trident, B star, C stripes

Page 44
Spot on!

A Turkey, B Azerbaijan, C Georgia, D Israel

Here's a clue

A Azerbaijan, B Lebanon, C Turkey, D Armenia

Page 45
All the elements

1 D, 2 C, 3 A, 4 B

Is it right?

C

Page 48
Camel races

A

Let's repair

1 B, 2 A, 3 E

Page 49
Sort it out

Turkmenistan: C, B, A
Oman: C, B, A

Quick quiz!

1 Red, white, green, and black
2 Pakistan
3 Carpet designs and olive branches
4 Mountains
5 Flag of Iran

Page 52
Ready to play

A India, B Bangladesh, C Bhutan, D Sri Lanka,
E Maldives

On the mountain

Page 53
Lost panda!

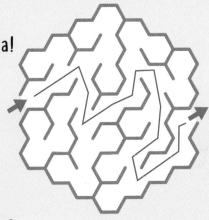

Which one?

Thailand: A
Mongolia: B

Page 56
At the temple

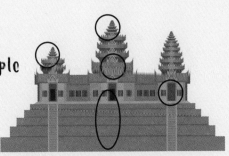

It's a puzzle

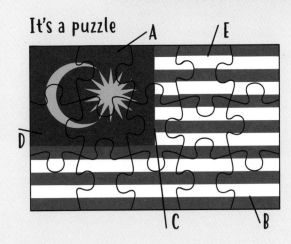

Page 57
In a row

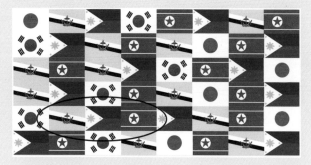

Let's climb
B

Page 60
Pyramid puzzle

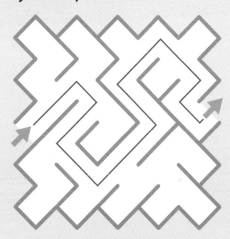

Birthday bunting

Page 61
Snip! Snip!

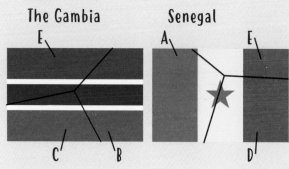

In a muddle
1 D, 2 C, 3 F

Page 64
Let's paint!

A Central African Republic, B South Sudan, C Djibouti

Let's race!

Winner: Niger = 22
Central African Republic = 17, Djibouti = 17,
South Sudan = 19

Page 65
Hubble, bubble!

A Côte D'Ivoire, B Liberia , C Togo, D Sierra Leone

Flag flying

A 2, B 3, C 4, D 1

Page 68
Match time

A–3 Cameroon, B–1 Nigeria, C–4 Equatorial
Guinea, D–2 Gabon

Mix-up!

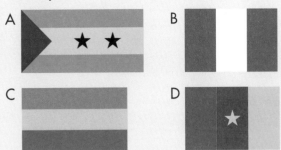

A B C D

Page 69
Ostrich race

A

Snap! Snap!

A Uganda, B Rwanda, C Kenya, D Democratic Republic of Congo, E Congo, F Burundi

Page 72
Rainbow flags

A Seychelles B Comoros C Mauritius

Impala puzzle

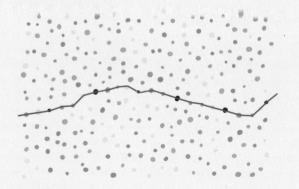

Page 73
Animal parade

D Elephant

Missing elements

1 C, 2 E, 3 A

Page 76
The right stripes

Venezuela C
Colombia A

Page 77
Llama lines

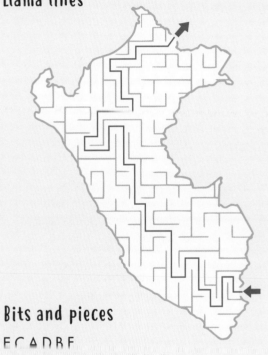

Bits and pieces

ECADBF

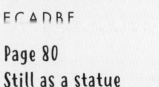

Page 80
Still as a statue

It's a puzzle

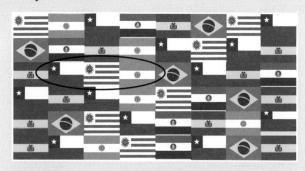

Page 81
Monkey mischief

A Uruguay, B Argentina, C Chile

Rally round!

Page 84
Aussie tour

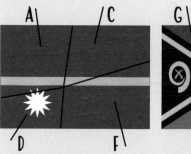

In paradise

E

Page 85
All calm

A Micronesia, B Marshall Islands, C Palau

Time to swim

A Marshall Islands, B Palau, C Micronesia,
D Papua New Guinea

Page 88
Snip! Snip!

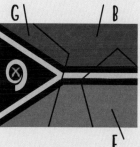

Fill me in

Page 89
Flying high

A

On your marks ...

A Samoa, B Tonga